SOPHIE'S TOM

Sanger

Sophie, though small,
was very determined.

SOPHIE'S TOM

DICK KING-SMITH

illustrated by
DAVID PARKINS

CANDLEWICK PRESS
CAMBRIDGE, MASSACHUSETTS

First U. S. paperback edition 1994
First published in Great Britain in 1991 by
Walker Books Ltd., London.

Library of Congress Cataloging-in-Publication Data

King-Smith, Dick.
Sophie's Tom / by Dick King-Smith;
illustrated by David Parkins.—1st U.S. ed.

Summary: Befriending a stray cat helps a very determined
five-year-old adjust to school, learn about friends,
and pursue her dream of one day becoming a
farmer. A sequel to "Sophie's Snail."
ISBN 1-56402-107-6 (hardcover)
ISBN 1-56402-373-7 (paperback)
[1. Cats—Fiction. 2. England—Fiction.]
I. Parkins, David, ill. II. Title.
PZ7.K5893Sp 1991 [Fic]—dc20 91-58756

2 4 6 8 10 9 7 5 3 1

Printed in Great Britain

The pictures in this book were done in pen and ink.

Candlewick Press
2067 Massachusetts Avenue
Cambridge, Massachusetts 02140

CONTENTS

*Sophie woke up early on the morning
of her fifth birthday.*

IN WHICH TOM APPEARS

Sophie woke up early on the morning of her fifth birthday. It was still very dark. Usually the first thing she did when she switched on the light was look at the pictures hanging on her bedroom walls. There were four of them, all drawn by Sophie's mother, who was clever at that sort of thing.

One was of a cow called Blossom, one was of two hens named April and May, the third of a Shetland pony called Shorty, and the fourth of a spotted pig by the name of Measles.

These were the animals that would one day belong to Sophie, for she was, she said, going to be a lady farmer when she grew up; and neither Sophie's mother and father nor her seven-year-old twin brothers, Matthew and Mark, doubted for one moment that she would.

Sophie, though small, was very determined.

But on this particular morning Sophie did not spare a glance for her portrait gallery. Instead, she scrambled to the end of her bed and peered over. And there it was!

"Yikes!" cried Sophie. "He came!" and she undid the safety pin that fastened the long bulging woolen stocking to the bedclothes.

By now Sophie was used to the fact that her birthday was on Christmas Day. The twins, who had been born in the spring, felt sorry for her.

"Poor old Sophie," said Matthew, "being born then."

"Hard luck on her," said Mark. "Glad we weren't."

But Sophie didn't mind.

"It's twice as nice," she said when anyone asked how she felt about it. "Everybody gives me two presents."

"It was clever of you, Mom," she had said to her mother once.

"What was?"

"Having me on Christmas Day. How did you manage it?"

"With difficulty. But you were the nicest possible Christmas present. Daddy and I both wanted a little girl very much."

"Why?"

"Well, we already had two boys, didn't we?"

"What would you have called me if I'd been a boy?"

"Noël, probably."

"Yuck!" said Sophie. "I'm glad I wasn't, then."

This Christmas Day, the sixth of Sophie's life, started in the usual way. As soon as the grandmother clock in the hall struck seven, the twins ran, and Sophie plodded, into their parents' bedroom, and they all climbed onto the big bed to show what Santa Claus had brought them.

Then, after breakfast, came the ceremony of giving presents.

This was always done in the same way. Everybody sat down, in the living room, of course—at least the two grown-ups sat down with their cups of coffee, while Matthew and Mark danced around with excitement, and their sister stood stolidly beside the Christmas tree, beneath which all the presents were arranged, and waited for the

*Matthew and Mark danced around, and Sophie
stood stolidly beside the Christmas tree.*

others to sing "Happy Birthday, dear Sophie, happy birthday to you!"

Then the opening of the presents began, one at a time, youngest first, oldest last—a Christmas present for Sophie, then one for Mark, then Matthew (ten minutes older), then Mommy, then Dad, and finally a birthday present for Sophie, before she began again on her next Christmas one.

This year, to Sophie's surprise and delight, word of her intention to be a lady farmer had somehow gotten around the entire family, and both her Christmas and her birthday presents reflected this.

From grandparents and aunts and uncles came picture books of farms and storybooks of farms and coloring books of farms. Best of all, from her mother and father, there was (for Christmas) a model farmyard with a cowshed and a barn and some post-and-rail fences and a duck pond made of a piece of glass in one corner and (for her birthday) lots of little model animals, cows and sheep and horses, some standing up, some lying down, and a fierce-looking bull, chickens, a turkey, some ducks for the pond, and even a spotted pig.

And as for her present from the twins—that was super, nothing less than a red tractor pulling a yellow trailer!

"The tractor's for your birthday," said Matthew.

"And the trailer's for Christmas," said Mark.

"What a lovely present!" said Sophie's mother.

"Yes," said the twins with one voice. "It was really expensive too."

Sophie felt a little guilty about this, since her Christmas present to them was the usual

"Yes," said the twins with one voice.
"It was really expensive too."

one—a Mars bar each, their favorite. Still, that was all she could manage when she had finished buying presents for her parents. Afterward she had unscrewed the plug in the tummy of her piggy bank, on whose side was stuck a notice that read:

FARM MUNNY
THANK YOU
SOPHIE

and found that there was only seven pence of her savings left.

At last there was only one present remaining at the foot of the tree, an ordinary white envelope with SOPHIE written on it. Underneath there was some joined-up writing that Sophie couldn't read. She had left it till last because it looked boring. Probably just an old Christmas card, she thought, as she picked it up and handed it to her father.

"What's it say, Daddy?" she asked.

"It says:

SOPHIE

Many happy returns of Christmas Day
Love from Aunt Al."

Aunt Al was Sophie's Great-great-aunt Alice, who was almost eighty-one years old and lived in the Highlands of Scotland. She had come to lunch one day in the summer, and she and Sophie had gotten along like a house on fire.

"Aren't you going to open it?" asked Sophie's mother.

"It's just a card, I guess," said Sophie, but inside the envelope was another, smaller, envelope marked Farm Money, and inside that was a five pound note.

16

"Yikes!" shouted Sophie. "I could buy a hen with that, a real one, I mean!"

"April," said Mark.

"Or May," said Matthew.

"You wait till you get your real farm," said Sophie's father. "This house would be full of animals if you had your way."

After lunch, Sophie set out her model farm on the living room floor. She loaded all the animals in turn onto the trailer, and then drove the tractor into the yard to unload and arrange them.

"You're lucky," she said, holding up the turkey. "We've just been eating one of your kind. Mind you, when I have real turkeys on my farm, I won't eat any of them."

"You going to be a vegetarian?" asked her mother.

"No," said Sophie, "but you can't eat your

17

friends. I will eat a stranger—from the supermarket."

"This farm of yours is just going to be a collection of pets," said her father, yawning in his armchair.

"That's right," said Sophie, "I like pets. I wish I had a pet now."

"You're much too young."

"I'm five."

"That's much too young," said the twins.

"I'll buy myself a pet, with Aunt Al's money."

"Don't be silly," said her father sleepily.

"I'm not silly."

"You are," said Matthew.

"I'm not."

"You are," said Mark.

"I AM NOT."

"Be quiet, Sophie," said her mother, "and play with your toy farm. Daddy wants to nap."

"You can't eat your friends," said Sophie.
"I will eat a stranger from the supermarket."

Sophie put the turkey down (on the duck pond, as it happened) and stamped out of the room. With hands rammed deep into the pockets of her jeans, she plodded out into the wintry yard, a short, stocky figure whose dark hair looked, as always, as though she had just come through a hedge backward. Her head was bent, there was a scowl on her round face, and as she walked along the path beside the stone wall, she mouthed the phrase that she always used to describe those who upset her.

"Silly, stupid, and sickening!" she muttered. "That's what they all are, silly, stupid, and sickening. Why can't I have a real live animal of my own—now?"

"Nee-ow?" said a voice above her head, and, looking up, Sophie saw a cat sitting on the wall. It was a jet-black cat with huge round orange eyes that stared down at her, and again it said, more confidently, "Nee-ow!"

Then it jumped down, trotted up to her with its tail held stiffly upright, and began to rub itself against her legs, purring like a steam engine.

Sophie's frown gave way to a huge grin as she stroked the gleaming sable fur. "Happy Christmas, my dear!" she said. "And how beautiful you are! I wonder who you belong to?"

"Yee-ew!" said the cat.

At least that's how it sounded to Sophie.

"You come along with me, my dear," said Sophie,
"and we'll see what we can find."

IN WHICH TOM
DISAPPEARS

Sophie's first thought was to get the cat something to eat. All animals must be regularly fed, she knew, and this one was sure to be hungry even though it looked sleek and healthy. Anyway, it was Christmas Day, when everybody eats more than they should.

"So you come along with me, my dear," said Sophie, "and we'll see what we can find."

She glanced at the living room window, but no one was looking out. They were all used to Sophie's tantrums, which did not really last long and were best left to blow themselves over. So she plodded around to the back of the house and in through the door that led to the kitchen. The cat followed close at heel, just as though it had been following Sophie all its life and just as though it knew what would happen next. It watched as Sophie opened the door of the fridge and pulled some bits of skin from the remains of the turkey. She put them on a saucer, with half a leftover sausage and some bits of bacon rind that her mother had put aside for the bird table.

"Help yourself," she said to the black cat. "Whatever your name is." She watched it eating.

"Actually," she said, "you should have a name, shouldn't you? Trouble is, I don't know if you're a boy or a girl, and you can't tell me, can you?"

"Nee-o," said the cat, raising its head from the empty saucer.

"I think you're a boy," said Sophie, "because you're greedy. So I will call you Tom." She took a milk bottle from the fridge and poured some into the saucer and some into a glass.

"Cheers, Tom!" said Sophie, and they both drank.

Her mother came into the kitchen.

"Sophie!" she said. "What on earth are you doing?"

"I'm giving my cat a drink of milk," said Sophie, reasonably.

"Your cat?"

"He says he's mine," said Sophie.

"Oh, don't be silly. It probably belongs to the people next door. No, come to think of it, they don't have a cat. It must be a stray."

"What's a stray?"

"A cat or a dog that's lost or hasn't got a home."

"Well, this one can't be a stray, Mommy," said Sophie, "because he's got a home."

"Where?"

"Here."

"Oh, no, he hasn't, my girl," said Sophie's mother firmly. "That cat goes straight out of this house, now, d'you understand? Daddy doesn't like cats, you know that. Anyway, it does not belong to you, it's got a perfectly good owner somewhere, and it will make its way back to its own house."

"How can he?" said Sophie. "He's lost. You said so."

The milk finished, the black cat rubbed its purring way around Sophie's mother's ankles, and automatically she bent to stroke it.

"I'm sorry, puss," she said, "but out you must go, and that is definite."

Black cats are lucky," said Sophie.

"Out!"

"Especially if they come to you from the right-hand side. Aunt Al told me that. And Tom did."

"Do as I say, Sophie. Take that cat outside," said Sophie's mother, bracing herself for a tantrum.

To her surprise Sophie simply said, "Okay, I'll just put my boots on and my coat—it's cold outside." When she had done so, she regarded her mother with a look of deep disapproval and added, "It's cold for cats too," and marched out, Tom following.

At the bottom of the yard was an old potting shed, where Sophie kept her flocks and herds—of such animals, that is, as she was allowed to own.

These included wood lice, centipedes, earthworms, earwigs, slugs, and snails,

The black cat hesitated on the threshold.

which lived in a variety of boxes, cans, and jars. Most were allowed to come and go as they pleased, and most went, but Sophie continually replaced the losses.

Now, out of sight of the house, Sophie opened the potting shed door and went in. The black cat hesitated on the threshold, but then, with the curiosity of all his kind, walked in. He jumped up on a large cardboard box—on the side of which was printed in black letters BAKED BEANS—sat down on the word SNALES, written in big red capitals, and proceeded to wash his face.

Sophie stood watching him. She was rubbing the tip of her nose, a sure sign of deep thought, and then said, "I've got it! Listen, Tom, you can stay here for a while. I'll bring you food—I bring cornflakes and cookie crumbs and cabbage leaves for these animals, anyway, so no one will notice. And you'll be quite safe—nobody comes down here in the winter—and I'll make you a nice warm bed."

First she closed the door and then she took a wooden seed tray off a shelf and lined it with an old burlap bag. Then she lifted the black cat, with difficulty, for he was quite heavy, and put him on the bag. But, with the contrariness of all his kind, he got out again and stood by the closed door, mewing.

"I'm sorry, my dear," said Sophie firmly, "but here you must stay, and that is definite. Now out of the way, please." But, with the disdain for authority of all his kind, the cat took no notice, continuing to mew at the door.

Sophie, however, was more than a match for him in determination.

"Do as I say, Tom," she ordered, and when he did not move, she picked him up, plonked him down facing the wrong way, and was out of the potting shed and had shut the door before he could do anything about it.

Later in the afternoon, they pulled crackers and put on paper hats. Then Sophie's father said, "What's this I hear about you bringing some stray cat into the house? Where is it now?"

Sophie disapproved of telling lies, and she had no intention of revealing the truth, so she said nothing.

"It's no good sulking," said her father.

"I am not sulking."

"She took it out into the yard," her mother said. "It's probably gone by now."

"Good," said her father. "You know I don't like cats."

"What kind of cat was it?" said Matthew, taking a huge bite of Christmas cake.

"A black one."

"Boy or girl?" said Mark, doing the same.

"Boy."

"How d'you know?" chorused the twins, with their mouths full.

"Because he bolts his food like you," said Sophie. "Boys are greedier than girls, everyone knows that."

She cut off a very small piece of cake.

"You should chew each mouthful thirty-two times," she said, and popped it in.

Like a pair of hawks, the twins watched the seemingly endless movement of her jaw, and the moment she swallowed, they shouted, "That was thirty-seven times!"

"Don't tease, boys," said their mother. "You know Sophie can only count to twenty."

Sophie was still sitting at the table when the rest of the family had finished lunch.

They supposed that it was the chewing that was taking her so long. But as soon as they had left the room, Sophie bolted what was on her plate, and then took off her paper hat and quickly wrapped up some leftovers in it. Carrying this parcel of food, she let herself out of the back door and plodded off into the twilit yard.

She opened the door of the potting shed a crack and called, "Tom! Here's your supper." But there was no mew from the dark interior.

Sophie opened the door a little wider and poked her head around. There was just enough light left to see the shapes of the boxes, cans, and jars that housed her flocks and herds, and the burlap-covered seed tray that was to have been Tom's bed. But there was no sign of the black cat himself.

Down on hands and knees, to make sure he

Sophie found a gap just wide enough
for a prisoner to escape.

wasn't hiding behind something, Sophie found a gap in the boards at the back where the wood was rotten, a gap just wide enough for a prisoner to escape.

Sophie felt terribly disappointed and sad. She had been so sure, in the short time that she had known the black cat, that theirs was a special sort of friendship, yet he had deserted her.

Some children might have given way to tears, but Sophie did not approve of crying. She was determined to look on the bright side. Tom had just gone for a walk. He would come back. He would need his supper.

She found a shallow flowerpot and tipped into it the mess of cake and marzipan and icing and cinnamon bun and peanut butter sandwich that she had brought. She filled a cookie tin from the old watering can that she kept there for dampening her slugs. Finally she propped the door of the potting shed ajar. Plodding back up the yard, Sophie called, "Tom! Tom! Where are you?" but there was no answer.

Early the next morning, Sophie went down to the shed, more than half hoping to find the black cat sheltering there. But a peep around the door showed only a fat mouse sitting in the flowerpot eating Christmas cake, and throughout the rest of the holidays there was no sign of Tom.

Sophie played happily enough with her toy farm, and only her mother wondered why she was quieter than usual. No one else noticed, for Sophie's father was back at work after the break, and Matthew and Mark were, as ever, perfectly content with each other's company.

It must be the prospect of starting school, her mother decided, that was making Sophie more than usually silent and solitary, spending so much time staring out into the garden. She was worried about meeting a lot of strange children—that must be it.

"You'll like school, you know," she said.

"I know," said Sophie. "I'm looking forward to it. They'll have farming lessons." She still firmly believed this, even though the twins had rolled their eyes and tapped their foreheads when she mentioned it.

Her mother paused in the task of trying to make some sort of order of Sophie's dark mop of unruly hair.

"You're not worried about anything, are you, darling?" she asked.

Sophie rubbed the tip of her nose.

"Only about Tom," she said after a while.

"Who's Tom?"

"My cat. You know."

"Oh, he'll be all right. Cats are good at taking care of themselves."

"I wish I could have taken care of him," Sophie said.

On the morning of the last Saturday of the holidays, Sophie had just finished a game of Happy Families with her father and her brothers, who had all agreed, rather unhappily, to play with her. She was driving her cows in for milking, when her mother returned from some shopping and stood on Sophie's right, looking down at the array of toy animals.

"School on Monday," she said.

"Yes," said Sophie. "I can do the morning milking before I go and the afternoon milking when I get back."

Her mother handed her something wrapped in a little twist of paper.

"What is it?" said Sophie.

"Just a little present. To bring you luck."

Sophie unwrapped it.

It was a tiny model cat, a black one, with big orange eyes.

"Why do I have to wear a skirt?" said Sophie.

IN WHICH SOPHIE
GOES TO SCHOOL

Every day of the two years that the twins had
been at school, Sophie had always gone too,
walking down with her mother or, if the
weather was horrible, going in the car. But
now, for the first time, she would not walk
or ride home again at a quarter to nine in the
morning.

Now, at last, she was a schoolgirl.

The day had not started well.

"Why do I have to wear a skirt?" said
Sophie.

"It's part of the school uniform," her
mother said. "You can't go dressed as you
like."

Sophie's usual clothes consisted of an old blue sweater with her name written on it in white letters, old jeans, and, most of the time, boots.

But this morning she stood in front of the mirror and saw a distinctly grumpy figure wearing a gray pleated skirt and, under a maroon cardigan, a gray shirt with a striped tie.

"These clothes are silly, stupid, and sickening!" she said.

"You look very nice," her mother said.

"You look very nice," her father said when she came down to breakfast. The twins said nothing (because they had been told to say nothing), but they looked at Sophie, and then looked at one another, and grinned. Sophie eyed their gray pants darkly.

"It's a pity you're not Scotch boys," she said.

"Why?"

"Then you'd have to wear skirts. They do. Aunt Al told me."

When they arrived at the school, Matthew and Mark galloped off without a backward look. Sophie and her mother made their way to the kindergarten classroom. Here they found a number of other children who were starting school for the first time. Most were clinging tightly to their mothers, some were sniveling, and one little boy was wailing loudly.

Sophie's mother glanced anxiously at her, but her daughter's only reaction was to pull down her dark eyebrows in a frown of disapproval.

"Imagine crying!" said Sophie.

"Let's hang up your jacket," said her mother. "There are some pegs in the corridor outside. Let's see if we can find yours."

If there was one word that Sophie was confident of reading it was her own name, and she had no trouble in spotting it. Beside each peg a child's name was printed on a picture of an animal—a lion, an elephant, a parrot, a rabbit. Sophie's picture was of a black-and-white cow with a big udder.

"Yikes!" said Sophie softly. "They knew!"

Sophie's mother felt that this might be a good moment to slip away. She kissed her, and said, a little tremulously, "See you later."

"Alligator," said Sophie in her usual no-nonsense way, and plodded back into the classroom.

It just so happened that the kindergarten teacher was also beginning her first year at the school, so that all the children, new and old alike, were strange to her.

Mostly they were strange to Sophie, too, as she sat where she had been told to sit and stared stonily at the others. Suddenly her expression changed from one of suspicion to one of active dislike.

Sitting on the other side of the room was a pretty little girl with golden hair done in pigtails that were tied with ribbon. This child, whose name was Dawn, Sophie had met once before, and an unhappy meeting it had been.

Dawn had been invited to Sophie's house to play, and had deliberately squashed one of Sophie's largest wood lice. In return, Sophie had taken Dawn's toy pony, a pink pony with a long silvery mane and tail, called Twinkletoes, and jumped up and down on it until it was a dirty squashed lump whose toes would never twinkle again.

Now, unaware of Sophie's sultry glare, Dawn chattered brightly with her friends, until the teacher called for quiet. Then the teacher told the new children that each of them would have an older child in the class to take care of them until they knew their way around the school.

"I know my way around," said Sophie.

"Do you?" said the teacher. "How clever of you . . . let me see, you are . . . ?"

"Sophie."

"How clever of you, Sophie. I guess you have an older sister in one of the other classes?"

"No."

"An older brother, then?"

"No."

Sophie loved guessing games.

"Go on," she said. "Try again."

"She's got *two* older brothers," piped up

Unaware of Sophie's sultry glare,
Dawn chattered brightly with her friends.

Dawn. "They're twins."

Sophie glowered furiously at her, but the teacher only said, "It's Dawn, isn't it? Yes, well, you seem to know all about Sophie's family, so you can take care of her."

"Yuck!" said Sophie, folding her arms and sticking out her lower lip, while the smug smile on Dawn's pretty little face vanished abruptly.

When the bell rang for morning break, the teacher made sure that each new child had an escort before letting the child go. Dawn, carrying a new blue pony, stood nervously in front of Sophie.

"D'you need to go to the bathroom?" she said.

"No," said Sophie.

She did—like crazy—but she had already determined that she would do nothing that Dawn suggested.

Out in the playground, the whole school ran screaming and yelling and skipping and jumping. The twins came to make sure (because they had been told to make sure) that Sophie was not unhappy.

They found her standing in a corner, glowering at the frenzied crowd. Nearby, but not too near, stood her caretaker, Dawn.

"You okay?" shouted Mark, and "You all right?" yelled Matthew.

Sophie nodded. Her expression, which was funereal, did not change.

The twins looked at Dawn, who was anxiously clutching the blue pony.

"What do you want?" they said together.

"I'm s'posed to be looking after her," Dawn said.

"She your friend?" said Matthew to Sophie.

"No."

"D'you want her hanging around?" said Mark.

"No."

"Well, get lost!" they both shouted and off Dawn ran.

Sophie began to jig from foot to foot.

Her brothers regarded her with practiced eyes.

"D'you need to go?" asked Mark.

"Yes."

"D'you know where to go?" asked Matthew.

"Yes."

"Well, go then!" they both said, and off Sophie ran.

One of the Bad Things that had worried Sophie about Going to School had been Having to Eat School Lunches, especially macaroni and cheese with tomatoes, which she hated, and at lunch time she plodded into the hall feeling sure that, today of all days, it would be just that. To her great delight, it was hot dogs and French fries and baked beans, followed by apple crumble and custard, both favorites of hers; and not even having to sit next to Dawn stopped her from enjoying her lunch very much.

From then on everything seemed to improve, for in the afternoon they drew pictures to take home and show their parents.

Sophie loved drawing. She worked away with her colored felt-tip pens, dark head bent, tongue sticking out with the effort. All the other children in the class drew pictures of their mothers or fathers, or sometimes of their houses, but Sophie's was quite different from the rest.

"What a lot of things you're putting in

your picture, Sophie," said the teacher when she came around to look. "What is it supposed to be?"

Sophie looked at her scornfully.

"Can't you see?" she said.

"Well, I wasn't quite sure ... "

"I'll show you," said Sophie, and with a red felt-tip pen she wrote across the top of the picture in big wobbly capitals:

MY FARM

"That's *very* good, Sophie," said the teacher. "Imagine your being able to write like that, and spell correctly too! You're a bright one! D'you think you'll be a writer when you grow up?"

"Of course not," said Sophie. "I'm going to be a lady farmer."

"What have you got there, Sophie?" said her mother when she came to pick her up. Sophie was carrying her drawing rolled into a scroll, with an elastic band around it.

"I did a picture," she said.

"Can I see?"

"When we get home, Mommy," Sophie said. "It's a present, you see. For you. And Daddy. And Matthew and Mark, I suppose."

"What's it of?" asked the twins.

"My farm."

"Your toy farm?"

"No, my real one, the one I'm going to buy with my Farm Money, when I'm a grown-up lady."

At home Sophie would not undo the scroll, but waited till her father had come home from work. Then the whole family gathered around the kitchen table for the Exhibition of Sophie's Picture, the result

*The whole family gathered around the kitchen table
for the Exhibition of Sophie's Picture.*

of her labors on her first day at school.

"That's very good, Sophie," said her father. "'My Farm,' eh?"

"No, mine," said Sophie.

"I was just reading out what you had written."

"It's beautiful," said her mother doubtfully.

But the twins were not prepared to leave it at that. They knew all about the animals that Sophie proposed to have, and they demanded to be shown the whereabouts in the picture of Blossom and April and May and Shorty and Measles the pig.

There seemed, however, to be a great many more animals in the picture than these—dozens, in fact, though it was anybody's guess which of the squiggly little figures were cows and which were hens or horses or pigs.

"What are those?" asked Matthew, pointing to a group in one corner.

"Pigs, of course," said Sophie.

"They look more like sheep," said Mark.

"Sophie's an impressionist," said her father, "and it's a great picture. But you seem to have an awful lot of animals on your farm, considering that you're planning to begin with just those five. How will you manage that?"

"I'll breed them, of course," said Sophie. "Farm animals have lots of babies. I thought you knew that."

"Yes. How silly of me."

"What's this little black thing here?" asked her mother, pointing.

"That's Tom."

"Your cat?"

"Yes."

"And what's this brown thing over here?" said Mark. "Like a pile of something."

"It is a pile of something," said Sophie. "It's the manure pile."

"Look," said Matthew. "There's a pair of legs sticking out of the top, as though someone had fallen in it head first.

"They have," said Sophie. "That's Dawn."

Dawn soon gave way to the disapproval
of the twins and the dislike of Sophie.

IN WHICH DUNCAN
COMES TO DINNER

Dawn soon gave way to the disapproval of the
twins and the dislike of Sophie. She sat by her
charge or lined up beside her when she was
told, but otherwise she steered well clear.

Sophie for her part was already looking
forward to the time, some two years ahead,
when she could do judo. She would throw
Dawn down on the mat with a terrible crash.

When the school year was two weeks old,
the headmistress was talking to the
kindergarten teacher about the new students,
asking how they were getting along.

"What about the twins' sister, Sophie?"
she said.

"Small but very determined," was the reply.

"How does she get along with the other children?"

"She didn't seem to think much of any of them to start with. I paired her off with Dawn, but that doesn't seem to have been a good move."

"A loner, is she?"

"She does keep herself to herself."

Sophie's mother was also worried.

"I know you don't like Dawn," she said, "but what about the other girls in your class?"

"I don't like any of them."

"The boys, then?"

"They're silly."

"All of them?"

"Duncan's all right."

Duncan, Sophie's mother found out later, was a very small boy, the smallest of all the children in Sophie's class. Sophie, she was told on asking the teacher, made use of him at playtime. Each held one end of a jump rope, and then Sophie stood still while Duncan moved in a circle around her.

"I was on playground duty today, watching them," the teacher said, "and she says to him, 'Walk on!' and 'Trot!' and 'Whoa!' just as though she was lunging a pony."

Shorty! thought Sophie's mother.

Indeed, when Duncan was pointed out to her, she could see that he might well have Shetland blood in his veins. He had a shaggy mane of ginger hair, short legs, and a fat stomach.

Not long after that, Sophie came home with another farmyard drawing. It was much like the first, including the little black figure of the cat Tom, but this time there were no legs sticking out of the manure pile. Instead, there was a short matchstick figure standing beside it.

"Who's that?" her mother asked.

"That's my farm laborer. He's throwing the cow muck on the pile."

"What's his name?"

"Duncan."

Sophie's new friend (or more accurately, it seemed, her slave, since he instantly obeyed every order that she gave him) had of course been spotted by the twins.

"Sophie's got a boyfriend," said Matthew that evening.

"Called Duncan," said Mark.

"He is not my boyfriend," said Sophie. "I've told him he can come to work for me. On my farm. When we are grown-ups."

"And what did he say to that?" asked Sophie's father.

"He said he would, of course."

"Of course. But how will you afford to pay him?"

"I won't."

"You mean he won't get any wages? He'll have to work for nothing?"

"Not for nothing," Sophie said. "He'll get his food. I've told him he can have free milk from my cows and free eggs from my hens and free cornflakes from my corn."

"Lucky boy!"

"He is," said Sophie, "I've told him so."

During vacation, Duncan came to dinner. Sophie had told him to ask his mother if he could, so of course he did; and then the two mothers fixed it between them,

"You have to be firm with earwigs," Sophie said.
"Don't stand for any nonsense."

remembering Sophie's instructions that he should bring his boots and that there should be cupcakes and chocolate Swiss roll.

Before dinner, she took him down to the potting shed to show him her flocks and herds. She was a little disappointed that he seemed nervous around them, especially the earwigs.

"They bite," Duncan said.

"Nonsense!" Sophie said. "You shouldn't be scared of animals if you're going to be a farm laborer."

She picked one out of the shoe box labeled YEAR WIGS.

"You have to be firm with them," she said. "Don't stand for any nonsense."

She pointed to the burlap-covered seed tray.

"That's my cat's bed," she said. "He's called Tom. He's very big and black."

Duncan did not look too happy about this news.

"Where is he?" he said.

"Oh, somewhere around," said Sophie, airily.

She did not notice that Duncan shot anxious glances around him as they made their way through the darkening yard. But no one could fail to notice that he enjoyed his dinner. As well as the cupcakes and the chocolate Swiss roll, there were sandwiches and soup and fruit, and the budding farm worker plowed his way through it all.

"He'll be sick," whispered Matthew.

"Or burst," whispered Mark.

"He's going to be very expensive for Sophie to feed," they said to one another.

Duncan was still eating when everyone else had finished, and might, it seemed, have gone on forever if Sophie hadn't told him to get up, they were going to play with her toy farm, he had to do the milking.

Later, when Duncan's mother had come to pick him up, they were standing at the front door, waving good-bye, when suddenly there was a terrible racket somewhere in the depths of the dark yard. It was a horrible yarring, yowling, whining, wailing chorus of dreadful voices, competing, it seemed, to see who could make the most awful noise.

"Yikes!" cried Sophie. "What's that?"

"Cats, fighting," said her mother.

"It might be Tom," Sophie said, and ran inside for a flashlight.

Though she would not have admitted it, Sophie felt a little scared as she crossed the lawn, shining her flashlight around, for it was very dark and the caterwauling was very eerie.

Suddenly there was an explosion of

In the light Sophie saw three dark shapes
rush across the grass.

spitting and snarling, and in the light Sophie saw no less than three dark shapes rush across the grass, over the wall, and away. All cats are gray at night, they say, but one of the shapes, Sophie was almost sure, looked really black.

"Tom!" she called. "Tom!" But the yard was silent now.

Not till Sophie had plodded back across the lawn and gone indoors did a distant voice answer.

"Yee-es?" it said enquiringly, but Sophie had shut the door.

*As soon as Sophie woke up, she jumped out
of the bed and went to her window.*

IN WHICH AUNT AL
HAS AN IDEA

"Why were those cats making all that noise?" Sophie asked later.

"Two toms, fighting, I guess," her father said.

"There's only one Tom—my one."

"All male cats are called toms."

"Why were they fighting?"

"Over a female, I would say."

"I bet my Tom won."

"I've told you before," her mother said, "he's not yours."

As soon as Sophie woke up the next morning, she jumped out of bed and went to her window. It was barely light, but she could see that there was a black cat sitting in the middle of the lawn, looking up at her window with his orange eyes.

Sophie crept downstairs and opened the back door, stuffing her feet into boots. She hurried to the lawn, but the cat had gone.

"Tom, Tom," she called, keeping her voice down so as not to wake the rest of the family, and to her joy a voice answered, "Yee-es?" At least, that's how it sounded to Sophie. Out of the shrubbery he came to be stroked, and then he followed her back into the kitchen.

"Have some milk, my dear," Sophie said, and filled a saucer, which Tom quickly emptied.

"Now listen, Tom," said Sophie. "You can't stay in the house, they'd only get angry, so I'll have to put you out again. But come back tomorrow morning and I'll give you some milk, understand?"

"Yee-es," said the cat.

And indeed it seemed that he did, for from now on he was waiting at the back door every morning.

"It's a funny thing," said Sophie's mother at breakfast one day, "but we seem to be using much more milk than usual. I keep having to ask the milkman for extra. Are you boys drinking more than you ordinarily do?"

"No," said the twins. "We don't really like the stuff, you know that, Mom."

"Sophie?"

Sophie stuck rigidly to the truth.

"I like milk," she said. "That's partly why I'm going to be a lady farmer. But I'm not drinking more than usual."

All might have been well if Sophie's father hadn't needed to go to Scotland on business.

"Sophie, get that animal out of here this minute!"

This meant catching an early train, and Tom was just enjoying his saucerful and Sophie was enjoying watching him, when her father came into the room.

"So that's where the extra milk is going!" he said. "Sophie, get that animal out of here this minute!"

"But Daddy—"

"No buts. Out!"

"Come, Tom," said Sophie with dignity. "Daddy doesn't like cats."

"I certainly don't like somebody else's cat drinking our milk," said her father. "Cats are only good for one thing, and that's catching mice. That cat does not come into this house again, Sophie, d'you understand?"

"Never?" said Sophie.

She looked so woebegone that her father relented a little.

"I'll tell you what," he said, "if ever

anyone sees a mouse in this house, then we'll think about having a cat."

"And don't think you can go putting saucers of milk out in the garden, Sophie," said her mother later, when she had heard all about it. "Cats should be given water to drink, anyway, milk just makes them fat. And that cat's fat enough already." She should have known that Sophie, though small, was very determined, and if she had been up early enough in the days that followed, she would have seen that Sophie had no intention of giving Tom up. She did not let him in, and she did not give him milk, but she saw to it that there were scraps of some kind put out for his breakfast every morning.

Soon it was plain that Tom had forsaken his owners, whoever they were. Whether they were unworried by his disappearance, or whether they had moved to another neighborhood, no one ever knew, but the black cat had clearly adopted Sophie's backyard as his territory and Sophie as his mistress. Now he even slept in the potting shed.

Sophie was delighted, of course. "If only Daddy liked cats," she thought. "If only we had mice in the house." But it was lovely to be continually meeting Tom in the garden, and lovely to be in bed at night and think of her black cat hunting in the black night outside.

"I bet Aunt Al will like you," she said to Tom. "Daddy's bringing her back with him, for a visit, when he comes home from Scotland. She lives in the Highlands, you know. They have Wild Cats there. Would you like to meet a Wild Cat?"

"Nee-o," said Tom.

When Aunt Al did arrive, apparently as fresh as a daisy after so long a journey, Sophie lost no time.

"Come and see Tom, Aunt Al," she said.

Aunt Al, small and birdlike with a sharp beaky nose, looked at Sophie with her head on one side.

"Who's Tom?" she said. "Your boyfriend?"

"No, that's Duncan," said Matthew.

"Tom's a cat," said Mark.

Aunt Al turned to her great-nephew.

"I thought you didn't like cats," she said.

"I don't," said Sophie's father. "And it is not allowed in the house."

"It's a stray," said Sophie's mother. "It seems to have adopted us. I've called the police and the SPCA, but no one has claimed it."

"They have," said Sophie. "I have. It's my cat."

*Aunt Al, small and birdlike, looked at
Sophie with her head on one side.*

Tom seemed to take to Aunt Al straight-away. He came out of the shrubbery and wrapped himself around her thin bird's legs and made his steam-engine noise. Aunt Al scratched the roots of his ears.

"So you can't come indoors?" she said.

"Nee-o," said Tom.

"Only if we have a mouse in the house, Daddy says," said Sophie.

"Which is highly unlikely, I suppose," said Aunt Al.

The very next day was one of those lovely mild early spring days full of promise, and in the afternoon Aunt Al and Sophie were walking around the yard together. Sophie was carrying the yellow bucket in which she collected fresh creatures for her flocks and herds, to replace those who had decided to leave.

They came to the potting shed, and there inside was Tom, crouching low.

"He's caught something," Aunt Al said, and sure enough there was a mouse between his forepaws, perhaps the same fat mouse that Sophie had found eating Christmas cake. It was alive and, though bedraggled, apparently unharmed, but every time it tried to crawl away, Tom raked it back.

"Poor mouse!" Sophie cried. "Let it go, Tom!" But the black cat only growled at her.

"Cats eat mice, you know," said Aunt Al. "It's quite natural. He won't let you take it away from him."

"He will!" said Sophie. "I'll make him!" and she moved toward him in a most determined manner, swinging her yellow bucket threateningly.

With a cry that sounded remarkably like "Yikes!" Tom shot out of the shed.

*With a cry that sounded remarkably
like "Yikes!" Tom shot out of the shed.*

"We can't just leave it here," said Sophie, looking at the mouse that was so shocked that it was too afraid to move. "Tom will come back. What shall we do, Aunt Al?"

"Just a minute," said Aunt Al. "Got an empty box somewhere? I've just had a great idea."

Thus it was that, later on, Sophie and her mother and her great-great-aunt were having tea in the kitchen, when Aunt Al suddenly said, "What was that?"

"What was what?" said Sophie's mother.

"I thought I heard a little scratching noise. As though there was a mouse somewhere in the room."

"There are no mice in this house," said Sophie's mother. "I can tell you that for sure."

"I'm certain I heard it," said Aunt Al. "Listen, there it is again!"

"It's over in that corner," Sophie said. "Somewhere by that old cardboard box."

Sophie's mother got up from the table and went over to the box and lifted the lid. Then she shut it again quickly.

"Oh!" she cried. "It is a mouse! Oh, I don't like mice! Sophie, take it out into the backyard."

When Sophie had done as she was told, she plodded back into the kitchen.

"Mommy," she said. "I told you what Daddy said, didn't I?"

"What?"

"'If ever anyone sees a mouse in this house,' he said, 'we'll think about having a cat.' So when Daddy comes back from work we can tell him we've seen a mouse, can't we?" Sophie's mother looked at them both,

the five-year-old and the eighty-one-year-old.
Their faces were expressionless.

Hers broke into a big smile.

"You wicked pair!" she said.

It was plain to everyone that, now and forever, he was Sophie's Tom.

IN WHICH DAWN
TAKES A TUMBLE

Tom proved himself to be a very tactful animal. He was careful not to take advantage of his new position as a house cat. He did not mew to be let in or out, he did not claw at curtains, or jump on chair covers with dirty feet, or worse. He did not make a nuisance of himself in any way.

He steered well clear of Sophie's father as though aware of his distaste for cats, and he kept away from the twins, suspecting that they might tease him. He was polite to Sophie's mother, but it was plain to everyone that, now and forever, he was Sophie's Tom.

Sophie, on the other hand, was not a

tactful person. Not content with being allowed to have Tom indoors, she demanded that he sleep on her bed.

"No," her mother said firmly. "Don't push your luck, Sophie. Daddy's being very good about all this, he's even having a cat-flap put in the back door; and I'm buying the cat food for Tom, and that's quite enough to start with."

Sophie, however, got her way in an unexpected fashion.

About a week after Aunt Al's visit, Sophie came home from school saying that her head itched.

"Where?" her mother asked.

"Everywhere in my hair," said Sophie, scratching away in her dark mop.

"Head lice, I'll bet," said Matthew.

"Or fleas from the cat," said Mark, and they beat a hasty retreat.

Later, when Sophie was in the bath, her mother noticed that there were spots on her back, dark, pink, flat spots, and she called the doctor.

"Keep her in bed for a while," the doctor said. "She's got a temperature. It's chicken pox."

"I haven't been near any chickens," Sophie said.

The doctor laughed.

"Try to keep her from scratching the spots," he said to Sophie's mother. "Anything you can think of to distract her? What does she like to do?"

"Draw," said her mother.

"And play with my cat," said Sophie.

"Good," said the doctor. "Well, you stay in bed for a couple of days, and have your cat with you, and then you can draw her."

"Him," said Sophie. " Bring Tom, please, Mommy."

"Only in the daytime," Sophie's mother said when the doctor had gone. "This cat goes outside at night."

But that didn't last long either. Sophie always left her bedroom door open, and Tom came in through the cat-flap as and when he pleased and sneaked upstairs like a shadow. And a rather fat shadow, too—he was getting positively tubby. Sophie woke up early each morning to feel the warm weight of him on her feet.

Apart from sitting for his portrait dozens of times, Tom proved a blessing during Sophie's chicken pox, for, whenever she felt she *had* to scratch her spots because they itched so much, she scratched Tom instead, and that of course he much enjoyed.

Meanwhile, at school, several other children in Sophie's class had caught chicken pox, though not, Sophie would have been sorry to hear, Dawn.

Dawn, moreover, was not slow to take advantage of Sophie's absence. She had not forgotten or forgiven the squashing of Twinkletoes, and now she deliberately set out to ensnare Sophie's future farm laborer. It was not difficult, for Duncan was not only a malleable little boy but very greedy. Regular offers of candy from Dawn quickly made him her slave, and he followed her around with the same doglike devotion he had once shown to Sophie.

Dawn should have known better. Setting herself up against Sophie was like a toy poodle challenging a bulldog, and she lived to regret it.

At recess on her first day back at school, Sophie went out into the playground carrying her jump rope. Part of the game she had invented, with herself as horsebreaker, was to go out into the paddock (the playground) and call the pony (Duncan). Then, when he came obediently trotting up, she would attach the tether (the jump rope) to his harness (hand), and the training would begin.

Now she plodded out again into the noisy throng of children and called, "Duncan! Duncan! Come on, come on, good boy!"

She had trained him to whinny in reply to this summons, but now she heard no answer. Then she saw, at the far end of the playground, a sight to make her blood boil. It was Dawn, lunging Duncan! In her left hand she held the blue toy pony, in her right the end of a jump rope, while Duncan marched solemnly around her.

Sophie plodded across the playground and stood just outside Duncan's circle, and glowered at Dawn.

"What are you doing with my pony?" she said.

Dawn waved the blue toy.

"It's not yours," she said, "it's mine, and don't you touch it or I'll tell the teacher."

"I don't mean that pony," said Sophie.

Duncan, meantime, having last received the command "Walk on!" walked on, and since Dawn was not turning with him, for she feared to take her eyes off Sophie, he walked in ever-decreasing circles, till at last the rope was wrapped tightly around Dawn's legs and Duncan was brought to a halt. Dawn was cocooned, like a big fly caught by a little spider.

Sophie stumped up to the two prisoners. "You," she said to Dawn, "are silly, stupid, and sickening," and she gave her a push in the chest so that they both fell down.

Sophie listened with pleasure to their howls, and then addressed her would-be farm laborer.

"And as for you," Sophie said
to Duncan, "you're fired!"

"And as for you," she said, "you're fired!"

"You should have seen it, Mom!" said the twins, when their mother came to pick up the three children after school.

"Dawn was bawling her head off!" said Mark.

"And Duncan was bawling his head off!" said Matthew.

"And the teacher on duty came up —"

"And said, 'What's going on?'—"

"And Dawn said, 'She pushed me'—"

"And the teacher said, 'Who pushed you?'—"

"And Dawn said, 'Sophie'—"

"And the teacher said, 'Did you Sophie?'—"

"And Sophie said, 'Yes'—"

"And the teacher said, 'Why?'—"

"And Sophie wouldn't answer."

"So what happened then?" asked their mother.

"Sophie had to go to the headmistress," said Matthew.

"In her office," said Mark.

"And what did the headmistress say?"

"We don't know," they said. "We listened at the keyhole, but we couldn't hear."

"What did she say, Sophie?" asked her mother.

"She said I was naughty."

"And what did you say?"

"Nothing."

"So what did she do?"

"Made me stay in all of the next recess," said Sophie. Then she grinned. "I drew a picture," she said.

Sophie took a piece of paper out of her satchel. It was one of her standard farmyard scenes, but this time there were two pairs of legs, one long and skinny, one short and fat, sticking out of the top of the manure pile.

*The twins' eighth birthday fell in late April, and
Sophie was busy thinking about what to get them.*

IN WHICH SOPHIE
GETS A SURPRISE

The twins' eighth birthday fell in late April, and Sophie was busy thinking about what to get them.

"It's difficult, you see," she said to Tom, "to know whether to buy them the same things, which is a little boring, or different things, when one might like his present more than the other."

She stroked his fat black stomach.

"What do you think?" she said, but he only purred.

She asked her father's opinion.

"I would ask them what they want," he said. So she did.

"What would you like for your birthday, Matthew?" she said to her elder brother.

"A radio-controlled model car," he said.

"And I want one too," said Mark.

"Oh," said Sophie. "What kind?"

"A Lamborghini," said Matthew.

"A Dune Buggy," said Mark.

"Oh," said Sophie.

"How much do they cost?" she said.

"About fifty pounds," they said.

"Fifty pounds for both?"

"No, fifty pounds each."

"Oh," said Sophie.

She took her Farm Money out of her piggy bank. There was Aunt Al's five pound note and quite a lot of coins that she had saved. She asked her mother to help count them.

"You have forty-seven pence there," her mother said. "So that's five pounds, forty-seven pence altogether."

"I don't think I can afford the kind of things the twins want," she said to Tom later.

"Nee-o."

"I guess I could cut the five pound note in half."

"Nee-o."

Sophie agreed with him. She was not stingy by nature, but that would have been overly generous.

"You're right, Tom. It'll have to be the forty-seven pence. And it'll have to be candy as usual. They like candy."

So next time they went shopping, she told her mother that she was going to spend forty-seven pence buying candy for the twins' birthday present.

In the shop, almost the first things to catch Sophie's eye were chocolate pennies.

"How much are those, Mommy?" she said.

Her mother looked.

"A penny each."

"So I could buy forty-seven of them?"

"Yes."

So she did.

Afterward she said, "Mommy, what's half of forty-seven pence?"

"Let's see . . . it's twenty-three and a half pence. Only there aren't halfpennies. If you wanted to split it, it would have to be twenty-four pence and twenty-three pence."

"Oh," said Sophie. "That's no good. They must have exactly the same number of chocolate pennies."

"Take one away," said her mother. "Then there'll be twenty-three for Matthew and twenty-three for Mark."

"Take one away? But what will I do with it?"

*"Open your mouth and shut your eyes,
and I'll give you something to make you wise."*

"Open your mouth and shut your eyes, and I'll give you something to make you wise."

After carefully dividing the chocolate pennies into two heaps (she could count to twenty-three now), Sophie had then put each heap into a little cardboard box, had written a twin's name on each box, and then put LOVE FROM SOPHIE on both. The boxes were part of a supply that she kept in the potting shed, but Matthew and Mark were not aware that they had once been used for keeping black beetles in.

When the day came, they were delighted with Sophie's presents.

"Gosh, thanks, Sophie!" they said.

"That's all right."

"Must have cost you an awful lot," they said.

"It did. Forty-seven pence."

By chance the birthday was on a Sunday, which meant that the children's father was at home, and what's more, it was a beautiful sunny spring day. Matthew and Mark had each been allowed to ask three friends to dinner, so they chose six boys with whom they regularly played soccer.

"Would you like to ask someone, Sophie?" her mother said.

"Darling Dawn?" said Mark.

"Or dearest Duncan?" said Matthew.

"Yuck!" said Sophie. "No, thanks. I'll just have my friend Tom."

"You give that cat too much food," her father said. "He's as fat as butter. He needs to get more exercise. Which reminds me — boys, do you want to have The Olympic Games again?"

"Oh yes, please, Dad!" they cried.

The previous year their father, who was fond of that kind of thing, had organized all sorts of running and jumping and throwing competitions, and they had called them "The Olympic Games." There were races, short ones across the lawn and long ones right around the garden, and high jump and long jump, and throwing the discus (a tin plate) and putting the shot (a brick).

So this year they did the same, and one or the other of the twins, who were good at that kind of thing, won nearly everything, or else tied for first place.

Sophie went in for every event and was always last because she was the smallest, but everyone cheered her for her determination. And in the last race of all, the marathon, everyone had to run six times around the garden while Sophie was allowed to run only three times, and she won!

Then they all ate an enormous dinner.

After all the guests had gone, Sophie plodded upstairs to play with her farm before bedtime. It had grown quite a bit since Christmas, for Sophie had either bought or been given a number of new animals, including a goat and some geese and a good many more cows. So big was it now that she had been allowed the use of the attic room at the top of the house so that the farm could be permanently laid out there on the floor. In the attic were some old pieces of furniture and various odds and ends, and there was even a scrap of carpet, grassy-green in color, on which the animals stood or lay or grazed.

Sophie knelt on the floor, the black cat purring at her side. With one hand she

"Time for milking," Sophie said.
"Time for bed," said her father.

stroked him, with the other she began to move the dairy herd.

"Time for milking," she said.

"Time for bed," said her father's voice.

He came in and sat down in a broken armchair.

"Come on, my old farmer," he said. "You must be tired, especially after winning a marathon."

"In a minute, Daddy, I've got to get the cows first."

She began to use both hands to pick them up, and Tom, released, jumped onto her father's lap. To her amazement, not only was he allowed to remain there, but her father was actually stroking him!

"Daddy!" she said. "I thought you didn't like cats!"

"I don't," he said. "Except this one. I've gotten used to him, I guess. You're a good boy, Tom, aren't you?"

"Nee-o," said the black cat.

"Oh, yes, you are. Come on, Sophie love. Beddy-bye."

As soon as she woke up the next morning, Sophie felt that something was different. What? Oh, yes, there was no black hot-water bottle on her feet. She got dressed and went out to see to her flocks and herds. There was no sign of Tom in the potting shed, or anywhere in the garden, and stranger still, he did not appear at breakfast time, which was when Sophie usually fed him.

By the time she had finished eating, Sophie was becoming quite worried, though she did not say anything to the others. She plodded upstairs to the attic to do the morning milking.

As she neared the door, she suddenly heard

some faint little squeaks. They seemed to be coming from the old armchair. Sophie went to look in it, and then she gave a cry of "Yikes!"

In the chair, snuggling against the now much smaller stomach of Tom, were four little furry bodies. One was tabby, one was tortoiseshell, one was black with a white bib and white feet, and the fourth was coal-black, just like its mother.

"Oh, Tom!" Sophie said. "How clever you are, my dear! And all this time I thought you were a boy. Whatever am I going to call you now?"

But the only answer was a loud, proud purr of contentment from Sophie's Tom.

DICK KING-SMITH is one of today's best-loved authors of books for children, including *All Pigs Are Beautiful*, illustrated by Anita Jeram; *Babe, the Gallant Pig*; and *Ace, the Very Important Pig*. A *Boston Globe-Horn Book* Honor Award winner and former farmer, he based the character of Sophie on a true lady farmer — his wife of fifty years. *Sophie's Tom* is the second story about spunky and stubborn Sophie, first introduced in *Sophie's Snail*. And her appealing, animal-acquiring adventures continue in *Sophie Hits Six* and *Sophie in the Saddle*.

DAVID PARKINS is also the illustrator of the picture books *No Problem* and *Tick-Tock* by Eileen Browne. His hobby is singing, and he is an accomplished tenor. *School Library Journal* has said of his illustrations for *Sophie's Tom* "Parkins has done bold ink sketches that are dramatic, lively, and striking through the use of contrast. They really show the characters' personalities."